BLACKSTONE PUBLIC LIBRARY
15 ST. PAUL STREET
BLACKSTONE, MA 01504

W9-CND-017

DISCARD

How to catch an Elephant

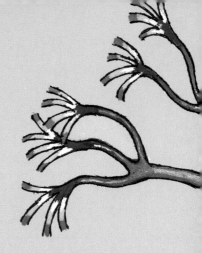

HOW TO CATCH AN ELEPHANT

Amy Schwartz

A DK INK BOOK
DK PUBLISHING, INC.

In memory
of my father,
Henry Schwartz,
who told me
this story.

3 cakes,
2 raisins,
1 telescope, and
a pair of tweezers.
That's what you need
to catch an elephant.

First, pack up your equipment.

Then, ask your Uncle Jack
to bring you to the place where elephants go.
On the way, he'll tell you three things.
"Remember, elephants are *crazy* about raisins,"
he'll say.
"And elephants *hate* cake.
And, in a pinch, don't forget your telescope."

Say thank you to your uncle
and wave good-bye.
Now you are alone.
Carefully
find a raisin in your pocket.
Place it on the first cake.
Now climb a tree
and wait
for an elephant.

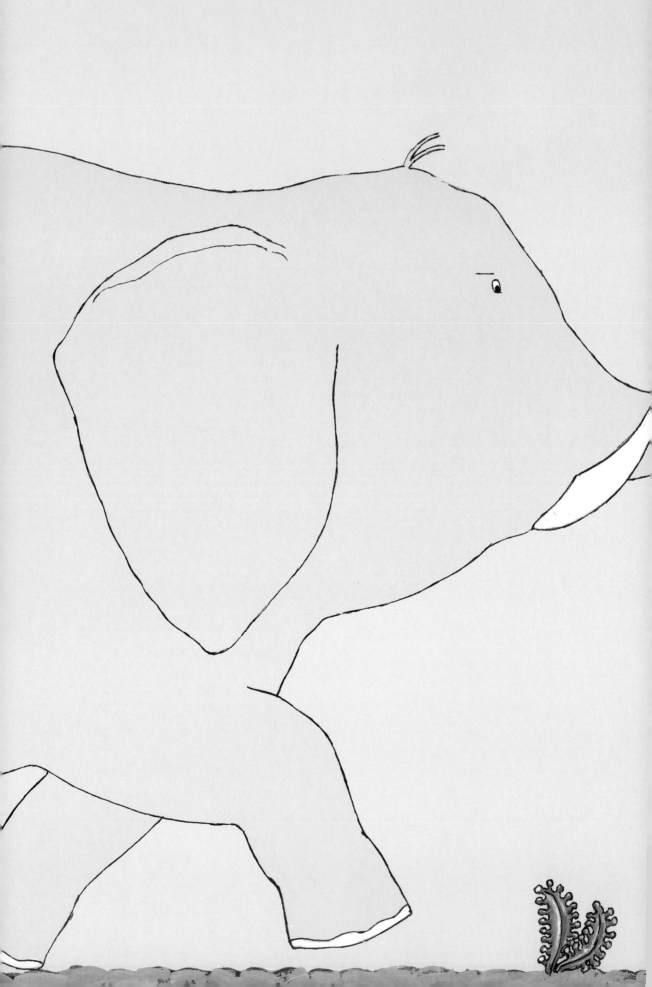

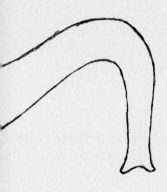

Stomp.
Stomp.
Stomp.
Sniff sniff sniff.
It's the elephant!
StompStompStompStompStomp!
He's smelled the raisin!
(Elephants are *crazy*
about raisins!)

He pops the raisin
into his mouth!

WHAT? No more raisins?

Only cake?!?

(Elephants hate cake.)

The elephant's great big ears flap back and forth.

His long trunk switches from side to side.

Stomp.

Stomp.

Stomp.

Stamp.

Stamp.

Stamp.

That cake is flatter than a pancake in Topeka.

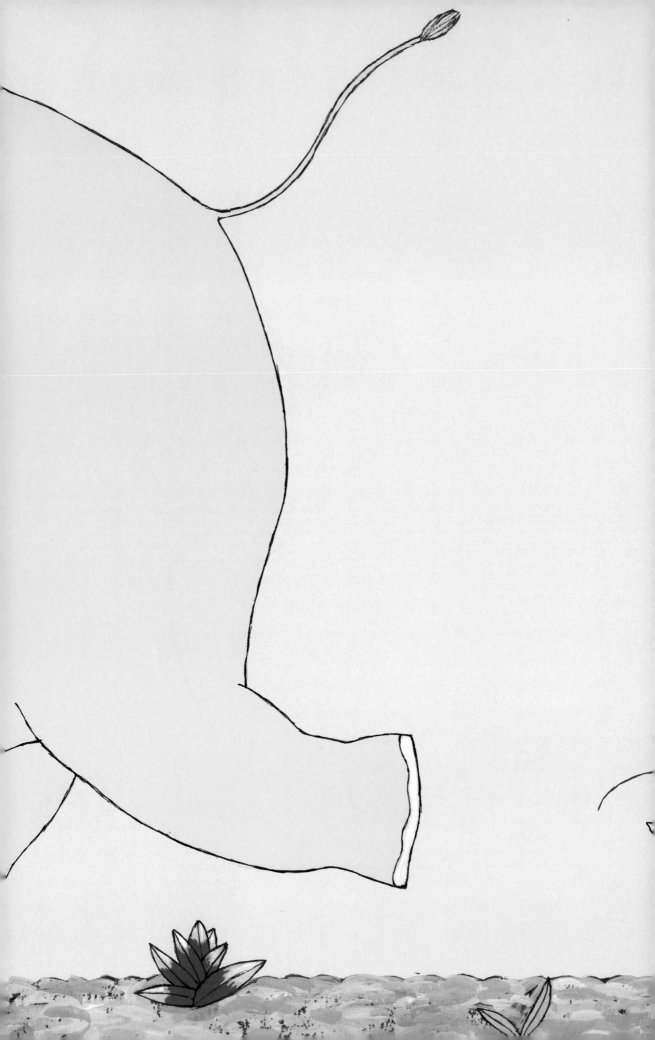

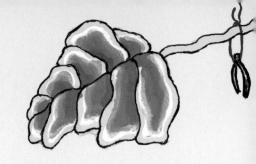

Make sure the elephant is gone.
Then, quickly, unpack the second cake.
Fish the second raisin out of your pocket
and put it on top.
Then scramble back up your tree
and wait.

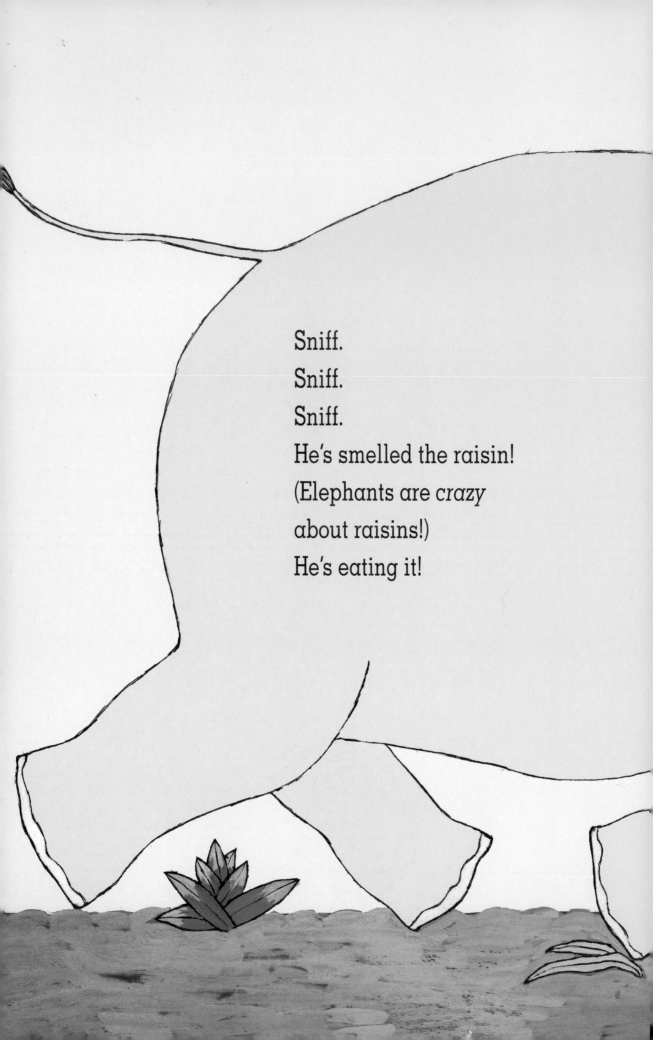

Sniff.
Sniff.
Sniff.
He's smelled the raisin!
(Elephants are crazy
about raisins!)
He's eating it!

WHAT?
NO MORE RAISINS?
ONLY CAKE?!?
(Elephants *hate* cake.)
The elephant's great big ears
flap back and forth.
His long trunk switches
from side to side.
He lifts his right feet,
and his left, and his right.
His whole body is twitching
and swaying
and he ROARS!

Be careful up in that tree!
Pray that you don't have any
cake crumbs on your fingers.

You are alone in the jungle with a very angry elephant.
StompStompStompStompStomp!
StompStompStompStompStomp!
That cake is flatter than a tortilla in Oaxaca.

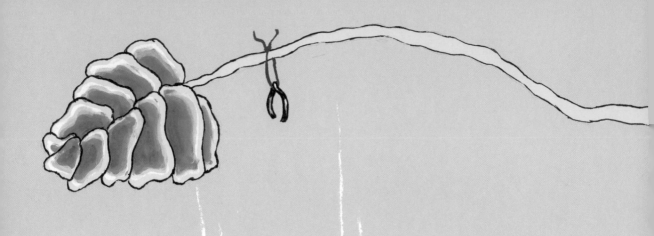

Open your eyes.

He's gone.

Fast. Jump down.

Take the last cake
out of its box.
Shimmy back up
to your branch.

StompStompStompStompStomp!

WHERE'S THE RAISIN?

Hold your breath! Hold on tight!

There are no raisins!

There is only cake!

That elephant was mad enough the first time,

he was mad enough the second time,

but now...

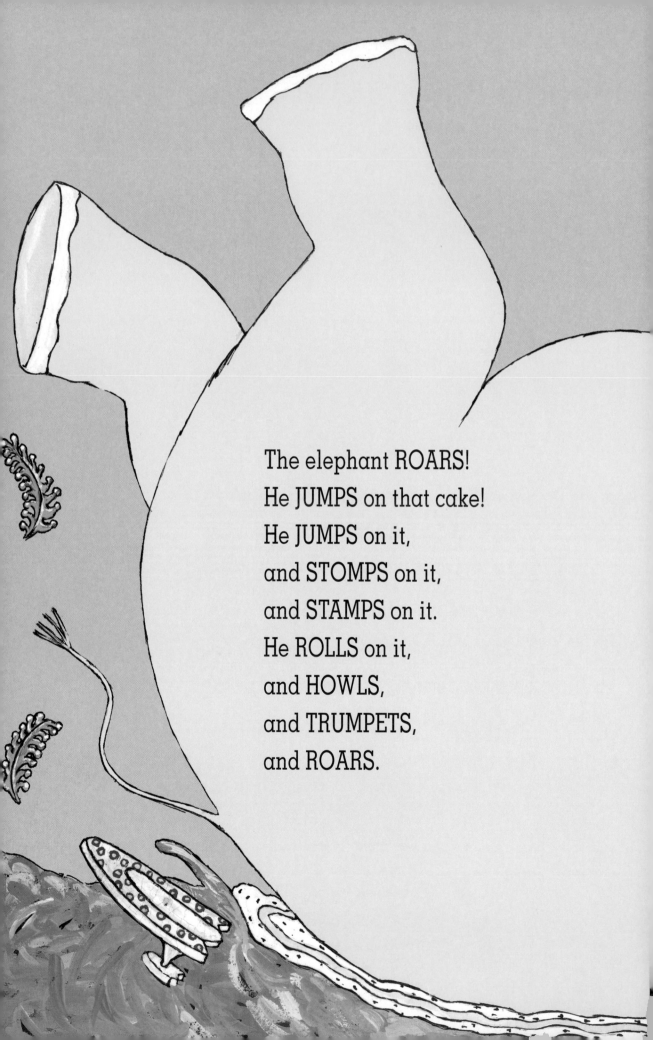

The elephant ROARS!
He JUMPS on that cake!
He JUMPS on it,
and STOMPS on it,
and STAMPS on it.
He ROLLS on it,
and HOWLS,
and TRUMPETS,
and ROARS.

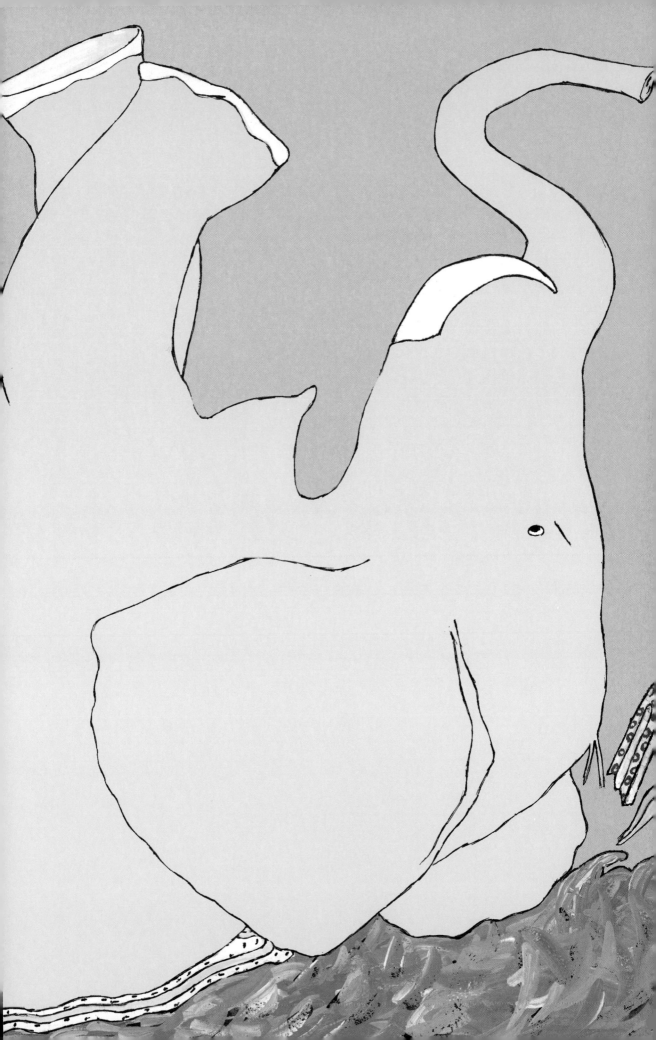

You are in a pinch!
Uncle Jack!

Help!

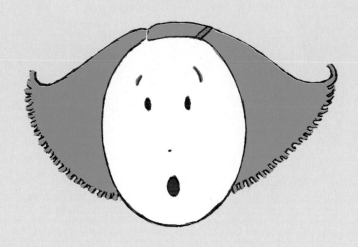

But wait...
Remember your telescope!

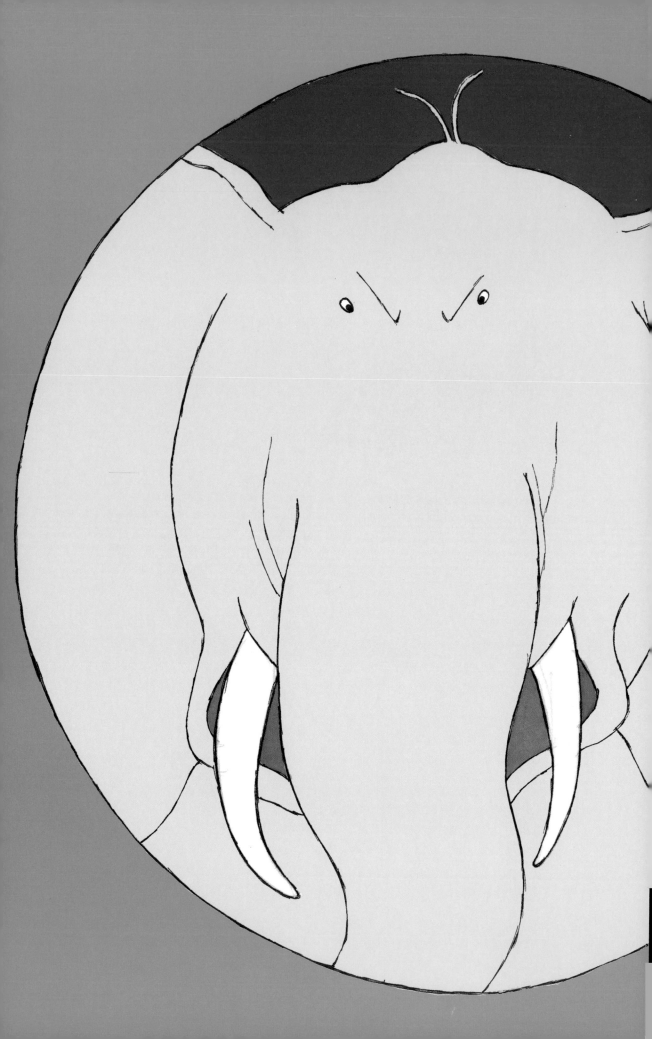

NO!
The other end!

That's right!
The wrong end!
Now the elephant is the size
of his *toenail*.
He is *teeny*.
Grab your tweezers!

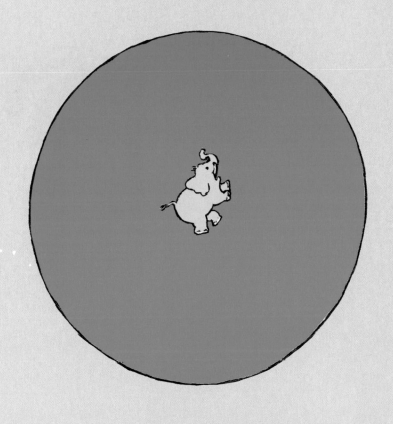

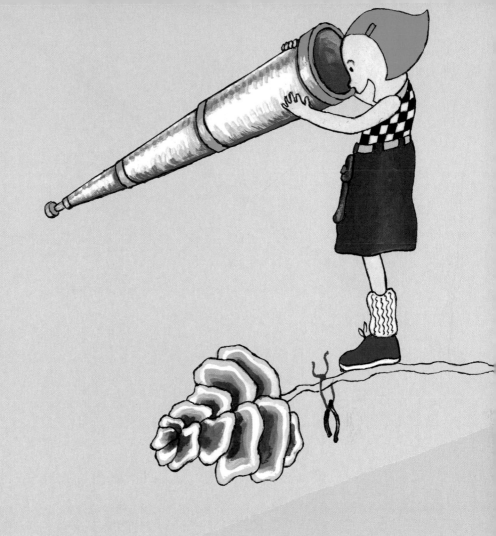

Climb down the tree.
Pick up that elephant,
and button him
in your pocket.

And that's how
to catch
an elephant.

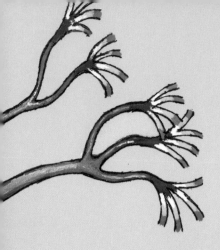

DK Publishing, Inc., 95 Madison Avenue, New York, New York 10016

Visit us on the World Wide Web at http://www.dk.com

Text and illustrations copyright © 1999 by Amy Schwartz

All rights reserved. No part of this publication may be reproduced or transmitted in any form or by any means,
electronic, photocopying, recording, or otherwise, without the prior written permission of the publisher.

Library of Congress Cataloging-in-Publication Data

Schwartz, Amy.

How to catch an elephant / Amy Schwartz. — 1st ed.

p. cm.

Summary: Provides instructions for using such necessary tools as
cakes, raisins, tweezers, and a telescope to catch an elephant.

ISBN 0-7894-2579-3 (HC) 0-7894-8185-5 (PB)

[1. Elephants—Fiction]   I. Title.

PZ7.S406Ho   1999   [E]—dc21   98-44864   CIP   AC

The illustrations for this book were painted with gouache.

The text of this book is set in 20 point Memphis.

First Paperback Edition, 2001

10 9 8 7 6 5 4 3 2 1

BLACKSTONE PUBLIC LIBRARY
15 ST. PAUL STREET
BLACKSTONE, MA 01504

DATE DUE

DEC 2 6 2003

JUN 0 7 2004

AUG 1 7 2004

NOV 1 6 2004

FEB 2 2 2005

MAY 0 6 2005

JUN 0 6 2005

AUG 2 3 2007

SEP 2 5 2007

APR 0 8 2008

NOV 1 0 2008

NOV 1 2 2022

NOV 2 2 2022

DISCARD

PRINTED IN U.S.A.

GAYLORD